The Surf Wave Lagoon

Carmel Reilly

Contents

The Surf Wave Lagoon

There is an outdoor surf wave **lagoon**
not far from the city.
The lagoon is like a swimming pool,
but it is only for surfing.

In a surf wave lagoon,
the waves are made by a machine.

Surfing at the lagoon is not like surfing
at a beach.
People go to the lagoon
because the waves never stop.
At the lagoon, a surfer can always
find a wave to ride.

There is a big building
in front of the surf wave lagoon.
The building has rooms
where people can leave their things
while they are surfing.

Next to these rooms, there is a cafe and a surf shop.
People may not have a **wetsuit**
or a **surfboard** of their own.
They can **rent** or buy these at the surf shop.

There are trees around the lagoon.

And there are places where people can sit down.

A Machine that Makes Waves

The waves in the surf wave lagoon
are made by a big, long machine.
The machine can make waves
that are high and fast.
It can make waves that are small and slow, too.

High, fast waves are good for people who know how to surf well.
Small, slow waves are better for children or beginners.

Big Waves for Doing Tricks

People who can surf well love going
to the surf wave lagoon.
They know that there will always be
big waves for them to ride there.

These surfers often go to the lagoon
to try out new tricks.
They practise tricks like jumping and turning,
and riding through big waves called barrels.

A Safe Place for Beginners

The surf wave lagoon is safe for beginners and people who do not surf often. They can practise for hours on their surfboards in the smaller waves.

People can take surfing lessons at the lagoon, too.
Classes are held every day
and anyone can come along.

Watching Family and Friends

Not everyone comes to the lagoon to surf or to take lessons. Some people just come to watch their family or friends surf.

People can buy food at the cafe near the lagoon.
Or, they can bring their own food
and have a picnic while they watch the surfers.

Festival Time

Big surf festivals are held
at the surf wave lagoon every year.

People come to watch the best surfers
show off their tricks.
There are food trucks and music, too.
It is a lot of fun.

The lagoon is a great place for anyone
who loves to surf or to watch other people surf.
This outdoor surf wave lagoon
has something for everyone.

Glossary

lagoon (*noun*)	a big pool that people can surf or swim in
rent (*verb*)	to pay money to borrow and use something
surfboard (*noun*)	a long board made from wood or plastic, used to ride waves
wetsuit (*noun*)	a rubber suit worn by swimmers and surfers to keep them warm in the water